for:

Maddie
noah
Otto
Arthur
Jacob
Mollie
Nancy
Belle
Sean
Owen
Evie
Amy
Jonas
Elsa
Jacob
Ruben
Edie
Beth
Sam
Charlie
Josie
Charlie
Ollie
Poppy
Freya
Jack
Hollie
Amalia
Theo

A catalogue record for this book
is available from the British Library.

ISBN 978-1-84780-084-8

The illustrations in this book
are pencil and pastel

Set in Myriad

Printed in Shenzhen, Guangdong,
China by C&C Offset in November 2010

1 3 5 7 9 8 6 4 2

First published in
Great Britain and
the USA in 2011
by Frances Lincoln
Children's Books,
4 Torriano Mews,
Torriano Avenue,
London NW5 2RZ
www.franceslincoln.com
All rights reserved

BATTY

Sarah Dyer

F

FRANCES LINCOLN
CHILDREN'S BOOKS

Batty isn't the most popular animal at the zoo. All he can do is hang upside down.

"hello"

TAPIRS

PENGUINS

WAY OUT

NEXT
FEEDING
TIME

His efforts to impress the visitors are always unnoticed. He is determined to try to be popular like the other animals.

LIONS

GIRAFFES

The penguins are having fun in their pool.
Batty wants to join them.

He
dives
in!

"Blerch"
splutters Batty.

The water is freezing and he realises that bats don't like fish. Being a penguin isn't such fun after all.

Next he comes to the gorillas. They look friendly.

Professor Boreal's
FLEA CIRCUS

Hmpf thinks Batty.

Perhaps they are a bit too friendly.
He is sure he doesn't have fleas.

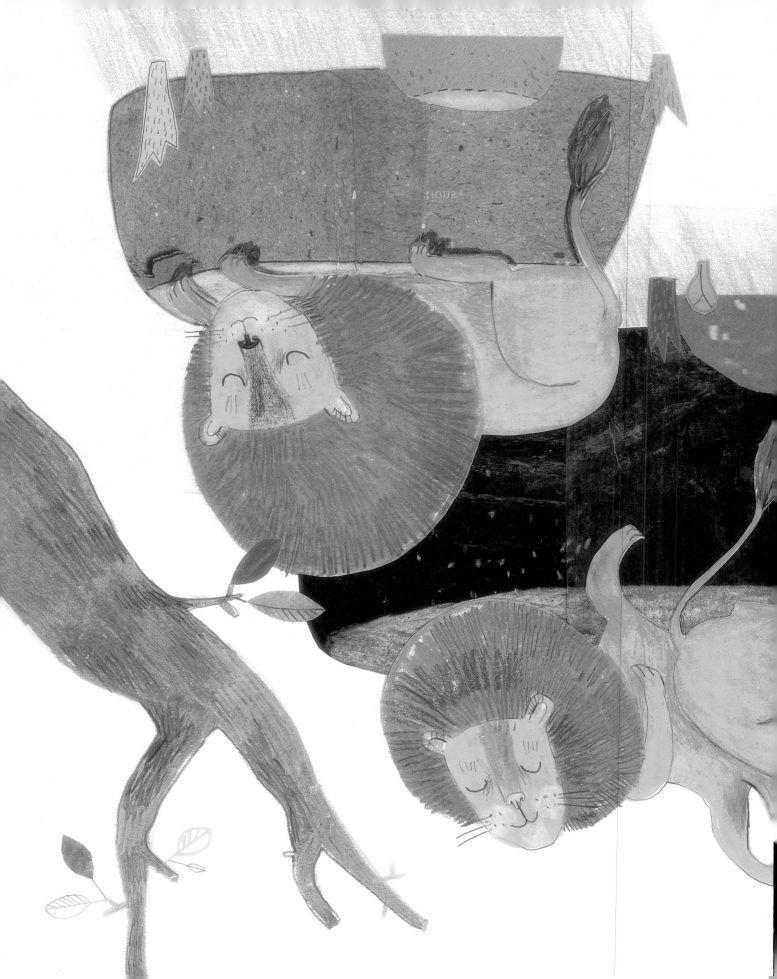

Moving on, Batty arrives
at the Lion's Den.
This looks very relaxing.

"*Phew!*" sighs Batty.

It is far too hot and bright in the sunshine for his tiny eyes.

tweeeeet

Not giving up, Batty lands
in the Tropical Aviary.
All the birds look so beautiful.

"Eeek," squeals Batty.

Up close it is far too noisy for his sensitive ears.

Feeling sad and lonely,
Batty flies back to his home.

When he gets there,
all the animals he has met
have come to visit him.
Batty realises that he is also
good at making friends.